REFLECTIONS OF THE ORB: A TALE OF MAGIC AND SACRIFICE

ATREYI ROY

Copyright © Atreyi Roy
All Rights Reserved.

This book has been self-published with all reasonable efforts taken to make the material error-free by the author. No part of this book shall be used, reproduced in any manner whatsoever without written permission from the author, except in the case of brief quotations embodied in critical articles and reviews.

The Author of this book is solely responsible and liable for its content including but not limited to the views, representations, descriptions, statements, information, opinions and references ["Content"]. The Content of this book shall not constitute or be construed or deemed to reflect the opinion or expression of the Publisher or Editor. Neither the Publisher nor Editor endorse or approve the Content of this book or guarantee the reliability, accuracy or completeness of the Content published herein and do not make any representations or warranties of any kind, express or implied, including but not limited to the implied warranties of merchantability, fitness for a particular purpose. The Publisher and Editor shall not be liable whatsoever for any errors, omissions, whether such errors or omissions result from negligence, accident, or any other cause or claims for loss or damages of any kind, including without limitation, indirect or consequential loss or damage arising out of use, inability to use, or about the reliability, accuracy or sufficiency of the information contained in this book.

Made with ❤ on the Notion Press Platform
www.notionpress.com

This is dedicated to all my dear **family members, friends and those who envisage magic in each second**. Let every smallest spark of imagination ignite adventure that surpasses belief. Do not stop dreaming; it is the only way to discover yourself.

All those who dare to dream, those who believe in the extraordinary things hidden in ordinary people, and those who embrace the magic that surrounds us every day.

This story is dedicated to travelers, dreamers, and believers—those who find courage in the face of doubt, strength in the bonds of family, and hope in the power of forgiveness. Always remember that in the pages of our lives there is a story full of love, laughter, and endless possibilities waiting to be written This story is for you—for your unwavering soul, your thoughtlessness mouth, and your desire to embark on a journey discovery.

With a heart filled with infinite gratitude and wonder,
Atreyi Roy

Contents

Foreword

Dear Reader,
As you embark on a journey through the pages of "Reflections of the Orb: A Tale of Magic and Sacrifice," allow me to offer a little insight into the world you are entering. In the heart of a bustling neighbourhood in 1985. Two siblings, William, and Charlotte, are about to discover that their ordinary lives are anything but ordinary Blessed—or perhaps cursed—with a mysterious sphere to fulfil their every wish, they are thrown out with a whirlwind of illusion. But with great power comes great responsibility, a lesson William and Charlotte learn as they navigate the challenges of their newfound power. Their every wish carries the unexpected, and they soon find themselves caught in a web of danger and deceit. As you follow the twins on their adventurous journey, you will discover the tried and tested relationship of family and the true meaning of **sacrifice**. Through trial and tribulation, they will discover that the greatest magic lies not in the power of the band, but in the strength of their love for each other. **"Reflections of the Orb" is not just about magic; It is a story about the power of choice, the resilience of the human spirit, and the enduring bonds of family.** My hope is that as you turn the pages of this book you will be transported to a world where anything is possible. So, dear reader, prepare to be amazed, prepare to be captivated, and most of all, prepare to believe in the magic that lies within you. You are in for an adventure,
Atreyi Roy

Preface

In the vast expanse of the human mind, there is a realm where the ordinary meets the extraordinary, where the simple becomes magical It is in this realm that "Reflections of the Orb: A Tale of Magic and Sacrifice" lies revealed—a parallel story with all the wonder and adventurous timeless charm of childhood. As the author and moderator of this story, I humbly invite you, dear reader, to journey alongside our heroes William and Charlotte as they navigate the wonderland of 1985. In community in the midst of so many, their unique motivation lies in travel—the mysterious sphere of their It has the power to fulfill every desire. But as William and Charlotte soon discover, the magical path is fraught with danger and uncertainty. With each of their wishes, they face the consequences of those wishes, leading to complications and surprising revelations. Through their trials, they discover that true happiness lies not in the imposition of external forces, but in the strength of their own hearts and the bonds of family that sustain them In creating this piece, I set out to weave a canvas of joy, mystery, and heartfelt emotion—a tapestry that speaks to the resilience of the human spirit and the enduring power of love. My hope is that as you embark on this literary journey, you will find a reflection of your own dreams, desires, and aspirations in these pages. So, dear reader, I invite you to suspend disbelief and embrace the miracle that lies within you. For in the pages of "Reflections of the Orb" the ordinary becomes extraordinary, and the impossible becomes possible.
With heartfelt greetings,
Atreyi Roy.

Acknowledgements

I extend my deepest gratitude to the remarkable advancements in artificial intelligence, which have greatly contributed to the creative process behind this story. The AI tools and technologies have been invaluable companions on this journey, assisting in refining concepts, and offering inspiration when needed most. Thank you for being my muse to the wind howling, the leaves rustling and the sunlight dancing through the trees. Thanks to the character of William and Charlotte for allowing us to embark on this amazing journey with you. Your courage, resilience, and unwavering spirit taught me valuable lessons about the power of determination and the beauty of friendship. On this journey that inspired the Magic Orb, thank you for giving me the gift of storytelling. You have opened my eyes to the infinite possibilities of the mind and reminded me that in every challenge lies an opportunity for growth and discovery And finally, thank you to all the Dreamers and Believers who have been with me on this amazing quest, thank you for your unwavering support and encouragement. Your faith in me has been a guiding light that has taken me through the darkest of nights and the brightest of days.
With boundless gratitude,
Atreyi Roy

Prologue

Built in 1985 in a bustling neighborhood where every corner holds a story and every street is alive with the vibrant rhythms of everyday life, a mystery woven into the fabric of life lies Lurking in the shadows of the forests are whisper the rustling leaves of ancient trees, beckoning the promise of mystery and magic. For siblings William and Charlotte, bound together by blood and passion, this simple evening holds the fruits of a different transformation. As the sun sinks lower in the horizon, casting a golden glow on the familiar paths, fate intervenes in the form of a mysterious stranger cloaked in shadows and wearing a glowing circle In a heartbeat, William's world shifts, and his consciousness is lifted by the vibrational energy emanating from the sphere. Little does he know that this chance meeting will unravel the seams of normality, unleash a series of events that will defy logic, and challenge reality As darkness descends on their family, the siblings find themselves trapped in a realm where realities are murky and dreams fly. Each time they step into the unknown, they are drawn deeper into the conspiracies woven by the mysterious circle, testing their kin bonds as they face forces that seek to rip their world apart. Thus begins the story of "Reflections of the Orb: A Tale of Magic and Sacrifice," where the line between reality and fantasy is blurred, revealing the true power of the human spirit in the midst of uncertain chaos revealed in the chaos of uncertainty Join William and Charlotte on a journey where each shadow holds a secret and every rumor Carries the burden of fate.

1

The Mysterious Encounter

Deep within the dense forest, where the sunlight struggled to penetrate the thick canopy, there roamed a boy named William. He was known throughout the village for his friendly demeanor and his insatiable curiosity. One day, as William ventured deeper into the woods, he stumbled upon a peculiar sight. A mysterious figure, cloaked in a dark robe, stood amidst the shadows. At his side were two imposing German Shepherds, their keen eyes scanning the surroundings. Yet, it was the luminous orb cradled in the man's hands that captured William's attention, beckoning him closer with its ethereal glow.

The stranger, noticing William's curiosity, hurried over and handed him the orb. "What's this?" William gasped, amazed by its shine and size.

"It's a magic orb," the stranger whispered, his voice serious. "It can grant any wish. But remember, it is immensely powerful, and you must use it wisely. And never, ever show it to a mirror. Bad things will happen if you do."
William, thrilled by the idea of having his wishes come true, rushed home, the stranger's warning almost forgotten. He hid the orb in an old box in his room, but the secret was too big to keep to himself.

2
The Magic Unleashed

He showed it to his twin sister, Charlotte, who was just as amazed.

Charlotte was cautious at first and suggested telling their parents. But William, eager to keep the magic to themselves, wished for something impossible to prove its power. Charlotte had failed her driving test, so William wished for her license, and in an instant, it appeared. The siblings were overjoyed and a little scared by the orb's power.

Their next wish was for invisibility, which they used to play a harmless prank on their mom, making her think they were outside when they were right in the room. For dinner, not wanting veggies, William wished for pizza, and the orb obliged, turning their meal into a feast of their favourite food.

Feeling adventurous, Charlotte suggested a trip to their favourite mall, 'The Dream'. The next morning, to their surprise, their parents announced they were all going there for a day out. At the mall, William, getting carried away, wished for the mall to be empty so they could have all the fun. But the wish went wrong – their parents vanished too, and they were locked inside.

In frustration, William threw the orb, and it accidentally hit a mirror.

3

The Mirror World

The orb came to life, angry at being used for selfish wishes. In the midst of the chaos at the mall, with the orb's malevolent magic at play, William faced a daunting challenge to save his sister, Charlotte, who was trapped in a mirror world by the orb. As the orb's voice echoed with menacing laughter, declaring the time limit for Charlotte's rescue, William's heart pounded with fear and determination. Charlotte's image flickered across numerous mirrors, her face etched with confusion and fear.

William, driven by a surge of adrenaline and brotherly love, began a frantic search. He darted from mirror to mirror, his hands trembling as he touched each reflective surface, hoping to find the right one. But with each failed attempt, a sense of desperation grew.

Time was slipping away, and William felt increasingly helpless. Just when he thought all hope was lost, he heard his parents' voices,from outside the mall banging on the doors of the mall. They had been searching for the kids after realizing they had disappeared. Breaking into the mall with the help of William, they were shocked to find him in such a panicked state.

Quickly, William explained the situation. Without hesitation, his parents joined the search. His father, Montague, took one side of the mall, while his mother, Anna, joined William. They worked systematically, touching each mirror, calling out Charlotte's name, their voices echoing through the deserted mall.

The orb, observing their efforts, decided to up the challenge. It announced that Charlotte would be shifted from one mirror to another every minute, making the task even more challenging. William, fuelled by desperation, doubled his efforts, running from one mirror to the next, his parents mirroring his actions.

In a stroke of luck, William, running towards the last mirror in a row, stumbled and fell forward, his hand accidently touching the mirror's surface. In that instant, a bright light flashed, and Charlotte tumbled out of the mirror, collapsing into William's arms.

4

Into the Orb's Depths

Overwhelmed with relief, William hugged his sister tightly, tears of joy and relief streaming down his face. Their parents, seeing Charlotte safe, rushed over, their expressions a mix of fury and concern. The family embraced, thankful for the reunion but aware that the danger posed by the orb was far from over.

This moment of William saving Charlotte highlighted not just his bravery but also the power of family unity in the face of adversity. With the orb still a threat, the family knew they had to confront it together to prevent further harm.

But the orb was not done. It absorbed William, challenging the family to save him within three days. After William was absorbed by the orb, Charlotte knew she had to act fast to save her brother. She remembered seeing a small hole in the orb earlier, which seemed like a keyhole. Determined, she told her parents about it, and they started searching for a key that could fit.

They found four keys, each marked with symbols of the elements: earth, fire, water, and air. Charlotte and her parents tried these keys on the orb, but none of them worked. Charlotte suspected these keys were just another trick by the orb to distract them.

She then remembered they had not checked one place – the janitor's closet. When she entered, the room was filled with a thick fog, making it hard to see. But Charlotte pushed forward, driven by her love for William. In the heart of the fog, she found another key, different from the others. When she touched it, she suddenly collapsed, overwhelmed by a mysterious energy.

Upon recovering, Charlotte took the key to the orb, hoping it would unlock it. Instead, the orb announced, "lock activated," confusing Charlotte even more. She noticed a new lock with a familiar symbol appeared on the orb with a symbol she did not recognize. She kept this discovery to herself, fearing she might have made things worse.

5

The Family's Resolve

The next morning, with the orb ominously reminding them of the time left, Charlotte sought out her mom, Anna. That is when she then noticed the tattoo on her mom's neck.After thinking about it ,she realized that she had seen that as a symbol on the new lock which appeared on the orb. Charlotte then ended up sharing everything with her mom, including the new lock and the symbol.

When inspecting the tattoo she got too close, upon touching the tatoo on Anna's neck, Charlotte was transported into a realm of her mother's memories. Here, she uncovered a deep connection between her mother and the orb. Anna, burdened by a long-hidden past linked to the orb.

She saw all her moms' memories floating all around her, every single one of them filled with happiness and joy. Upon looking further into all the memories, she encoutered a door. It was semi-broken and was close. There was a small sign on it which mentioned "Forgotten Memories." Once she opened the door she saw an unfamiliar face. This unknown person and her mom were playing like loving devoted siblings. Jumping up and down and having fun. Then came a flashing light and all the laughter stopped. It went black. Then Charlotte saw the orb from a distance and everything turned into a fog. She came back to the real world.

Realizing the truth, Charlotte called for a family meeting to discuss their next steps. It was clear that Anna had some past links to the orb and hence was the key to saving William. They didn't know how to though.

Upon aksing the orb , the orb replied " she must sacrifice herself for one to be free." The family was torn. Charlotte did not want to lose her mom, but Anna was resolute. She explained that as a mother, her children's safety was her utmost priority, and if sacrificing herself would save William, then she was prepared to do so.

With heavy hearts, the family agreed to Anna's plan. They gathered around the orb, each grappling with the emotions of the moment. Anna, with a mother's courage, stepped forward to fulfil her role as the key, ready to make the ultimate sacrifice for her son's freedom. The air was thick with tension and love as Anna prepared to unlock the orb and bring William back to them.

6

A Miraculous Reunion

Then, as the light fades, a miraculous scene unfolds. William, looking bewildered but unharmed, steps out from where the orb once was. Beside him is Anna, safe and sound, her sacrifice having unlocked the orb's final mystery. But there's another figure emerging from the light—a woman unfamiliar to Charlotte and Montague but instantly recognized by Anna. It's Susie, Anna's long-lost friend, whose own entanglement with the orb had been a dark chapter in its history.

The room erupts into a cacophony of emotions. Charlotte and Montague rush forward, their relief and joy overwhelming as they embrace William and Anna. Tears, laughter, and a flurry of questions fill the air as they try to make sense of the impossible reunion.

Susie, as it turns out, was a childhood friend of Anna Capulet. Both Susie and Anna grew up in the same orphanage, sharing a bond as strong as sisters. Their lives took a dramatic turn when they were adopted by a kind couple, Jack and Jacqueline, who showered them with love and care. However, Susie always felt overshadowed by Anna, believing the couple favored her more.

In her longing for attention and love, Susie stumbled upon the orb. Unaware of its true power and the grave warning to never expose it to a mirror, she made a wish that would change their lives forever. She wished for something selfish—the disappearance of Anna—hoping it would make her feel more loved and appreciated. But the moment the orb's reflection caught in a mirror while playing outside with Anna, a catastrophic event was triggered, and Susie was absorbed into the orb, becoming a part of its magical essence. This traumatic event impacted Anna deeply, forcing her to forget it.

For years, Susie remained trapped within the orb, her existence erased from the world as if she had never been a part of it. The orb, now cursed with Susie's unfulfilled desires and resentment, wandered through time, passing from one unsuspecting keeper to another, until it found its way to William.

The revelation of Susie's fate explains the orb's vengeful behavior and its desire to inflict consequences on those who wielded its power without heed. Anna, upon realizing the connection and remembering her long-lost friend, understood that she was the key to breaking the cycle. Her pure soul and the deep bond she once shared with Susie were what the orb sought to free itself and Susie from the torment of unfulfilled wishes.

As the friends and family stand together, absorbing the magnitude of what has happened, Anna steps forward, reaching out to Susie. With tears in her eyes, she whispers, "I'm so sorry, Susie. I never forgot you."

Susie, with a tearful smile, responds, "It was never your fault, Anna. I was lost, but now I'm found." The room, once filled with tension and sorrow, now holds an air of hope and forgiveness. The orb, now devoid of its curse, dissolves into a shower of light, signifying the end of its long, dark journey.

7

Forgiveness and New Beginnings

Now they included Susie, and their relationship was stronger and they were more united than ever. They learned valuable lessons about the power of wishes, the importance of responsibility, and most importantly, the healing power of forgiveness and love. The orb, its purpose fulfilled, became dormant, a silent reminder of their incredible journey and the magic that binds them together.

Glossary

Bustling: (adjective) *A place or situation that is full of energetic and noisy activity, often with people moving around quickly.*

Lively: (adjective) *Full of life and energy.*

Cloaked: (adjective) *Covered or concealed, often with a garment like a cloak.*

German Shepherds: (noun) *A breed of large, strong, and intelligent dogs often used for herding and protection. (Proper noun: German Shepherds refers to the specific breed of dog.)*

Orb: (noun) *A spherical object, often referring to a celestial body like a planet or a spherical-shaped artifact.*

Dense: (adjective) *Closely compacted together, usually referring to something like foliage or a forest.*

Canopy: (noun) *The upper layer of branches and leaves formed by trees in a forest.*

Peculiar: (adjective) *Strange or unusual.*

Figure: (noun) *A person, especially one of unspecified identity or importance.*

Imposing: (adjective): *Impressive and commanding attention or respect.*

Ethereal: (adjective) *Delicate and otherworldly in a way that seems too perfect for this world.*

Desperation: (noun) *A state of despair, typically resulting from a feeling of helplessness or desperation.*

Adrenaline: (noun) *A hormone secreted by the adrenal glands, especially in conditions of stress, increasing rates of blood circulation, breathing, and preparing muscles for exertion.*

Miraculous: (adjective) *Highly improbable and extraordinary, bringing very welcome consequences.*

Cacophony: (noun) *A harsh, discordant mixture of sounds.*

Incredulous: (adjective) *Unwilling or unable to believe something.*

Orphanage: (noun) *A residential institution for the care and education of orphans.*

Entanglement: (noun) *The action or fact of entangling or being entangled.*

Catastrophic: (adjective) *Involving or causing sudden great damage or suffering.*

Bittersweet: (adjective) *Arousing pleasure tinged with sadness or pain.*

Appendix

In the world of "Reflections of the Orb: A Tale of Magic and Sacrifice," there are several magical terms and concepts that have important bearings on the story. Here we delve into some of the key magical terms to help the reader know their views and understanding:

The Orb: A mysterious orb is a strong magical artifact to which any wish granted is made by its owner. It's an ancient artifact but commands great power, but there are consequences attached.

Wish Fulfillment: The magic orb is said to grant the wishes of its bearer or their requests. The magic orb tends to grant almost any wish without fail; however, the consequences emanating from these wishes depend on the type of wish and the good intentions behind it.

Mirror Magic: A special feature of the power that the orb has is that it is connected to mirrors. When the reflection of the orb is exposed to a mirror, it can trigger unpredictable and sometimes dangerous magical effects. This feature serves as the central plot element, driving much of the conflict and suspense in the story.

Consequences: Each wish made with the orb bears consequences, whether it be intended or unintended. These can range from minor inconvenience to significant disruptions in reality. In the story, characters learn about responsibility and accountability when they confront the fallout of their wishes.

Family Unity: A recurring theme in the story is the role played by family unity and support in facing the trials of life. The siblings, William and Charlotte, along with the love and sacrifice given by their parents, Anna and Montague, are also key in pushing through the fear of the orb to conclude that they have just been saved from harm.

www.ingramcontent.com/pod-product-compliance
Lightning Source LLC
Chambersburg PA
CBHW040901110726

48005CB00001B/157